I0722707

"A dog that's not a bitch is not a dog."

Old Romanian Saying

MOM

A DOG STORY PREQUEL TO BECOMING K-9

RADA JONES

APOLODOR

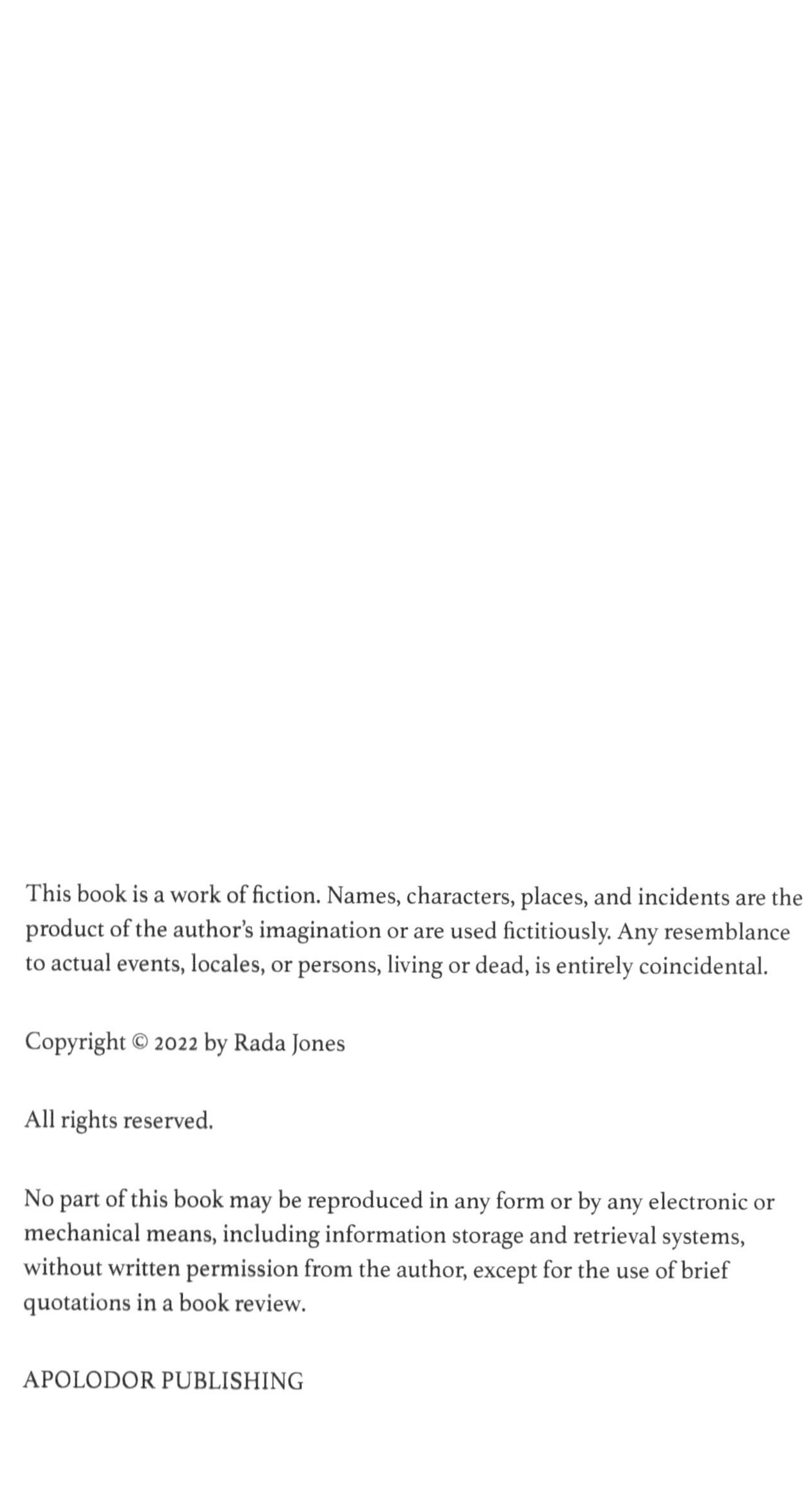

MOM

1

—————

THE PUPPIES' BIRTH

I glimpse something moving, and I take off in hot pursuit. I push away the leaf-covered ground and fly over a dead tree trunk like a bird. My tail slices the air, giving me direction as my front paws hit the ground. I scatter the dry leaves with my muzzle and sniff a musty whiff of mud and mushrooms. I plant my feet to leap again, but Gun's dark shape flies past me like a hawk, and the squirrel screams. My insides twist with pain.

Gun caught it? But he never...

Another twist of pain, and I open my eyes to Jones's bedroom. It was just a dream. I'm no longer Maddie, the young pup chasing squirrels with my brother Gun. That was years ago. I'm almost an old lady these days. My full name is Madeline Rose Kahn Van Jones, but I prefer to be called Mom.

I get up to check on things like I always do. It's my job.

Outside the arched windows, lit by the full moon, the maples throw twisted dark shadows. They'd be menacing if I didn't know every inch of this place. But I do, and I know it's all like it should be. My memory-foam bed; the smell of Dove soap, cigar smoke, and beer; Jones's light snore as he lays on his back; the shiny wooden floors smelling like Bona.

Good. I curl back in my bed when something inside me rips apart, taking my breath away. I yelp in pain. It's like my belly took a life of its own. It squeezes and churns and tries to turn itself inside out.

Jones sits up and shakes his head to clear it.

"What's up, Maddie? Is it time? I thought we had a few more days!"

He turns on the light and fumbles for his glasses, then throws off his cover and comes to kneel by my bed. He lays his gnarled hands on my stormy belly and gasps.

"Yep. It's time, old girl. Take it easy, sweetheart. You know how to do this. You've done it before."

Sure, I have. Five times, in fact. This is my sixth litter. It hurts, but I'm not scared. It's just a matter of time before my puppies come out, and there's no greater joy. I can't wait to meet them.

My insides squeeze again, and I need to push. Jones's hands cup my belly, his teary eyes watching my tail so intently they're ready to pop out.

"The first one's coming! Push, Maddie, push!"

Like I need him to tell me! I hold my breath and push with all I've got. Jones lifts my tail to look under it.

"Wow, Maddie! You're doing great, but this one's big! Just one more push, baby!"

I push again, but nothing happens. He lied like humans always do.

"One more, Maddie. You can do that."

I want to growl to shut him up, but I don't have any spare energy. So I take a deep breath and push like my life depends on it. A stab of searing pain, then the pressure releases, and Number One pops out.

Jones sighs.

"Good job, Maddie. There he is."

He picks him up and sets him under my nose. I sniff him carefully. He's just a dark, slippery blob, but he wiggles, and I fall in love. I lick him clean, loving every inch of him and soothing him as he squeaks like a field mouse. He's not much bigger than that and only half that pretty, but to me, he's the cutest creature in the world. I know he's bald, deaf, and blind, but he's my baby, and that's all that matters.

"Good job, Maddie. This one is gonna be Blue."

Jones wraps a tiny blue collar around his neck and hands him back. I'm about to give him a second bath when a horrendous cramp takes my breath away.

"Another one coming," Jones says, staring under my tail.

Thanks for letting me know, I want to growl, but I save my breath to push. Seconds later, Number Two pops out.

"This one's gonna be Green. She looks perfect," Jones mutters, putting on her collar.

I inspect her, then clean up every nook and cranny before proceeding to deliver Brown, White, Black, and finally Yellow.

My heart bursts with love. Jones cleans his foggy glasses with the sleeve of his pajamas, then picks them up one by one, looks under their tails, counts their toes, and sets them on my belly. One by one, they sniff their way to the milk bar, latch on, and start feeding.

I'm ecstatic. Exhausted too, but that doesn't matter. All that matters is that my pups are here, and I love them more than I thought I could. My world is so full of love I'm afraid my heart will burst.

Jones pets my head and kisses my nose. He's all sweaty and flushed with pride, like a new dad, and his eyes sparkle behind his round glasses as he watches them feed.

"Good job, Maddie. You got six, three boys and three girls, and they all look healthy and strong."

He brings a bowl of ice water. I lap it, then lay on my side to watch the puppies feed. But suddenly, something feels wrong. I need to get up and pace, and I must do it now.

I scramble to my paws. The puppies fall off the milk bar like ripe fruit. They squeak and pile over each other, mad the dinner service is over. But I can't help them right now.

I start pacing.

Jones frowns.

"What's up, Maddie? Are you OK?"

2

THE RUNT OF THE LITTER

Am I OK? Are you kidding? Anything but.

I shake my head.

"No."

I feel something's wrong, but I can't put my paw on it. So I start pacing back and forth, avoiding the squirm of squeaky puppies trying to crawl to me.

Jones gathers them and puts them in my bed. They scream to high heaven, breaking my heart, but I can't help them. I need to pace. I don't know why, but it's like my life depends on it.

I walk from the door to the window and back, again and again, panting with my tongue to my knees.

A massive cramp tears me apart.

I yelp, squat, and push as hard as I can.

Jones kneels next to me, his old eyes worried.

"You OK, baby? What's going on, Maddie? You've got another one? Hang in there, sweetheart."

I push through the pain tearing me up inside. It hurts, but

I can't stop now. I hold my breath and push again, then yelp in pain when the last pup comes out. Thank Dog.

I check her out. She's dark, gooey, and slippery like the others, but this one doesn't wiggle.

I lick her clean, clearing her nose and mouth like I did with the others, but she doesn't move. She just lays there with her little blue tongue popping out of her mouth. She's not breathing.

A stab of pain freezes my heart, and I'm scared. I've never seen this before. What do I do?

I pick her up and drop her on the floor to wake her up, but she doesn't wake up. She doesn't even squeak. She just lays limp.

That can't be! Not my baby! I cry my pain and lick her again. Jones reaches for her.

"Let me have her."

He takes off his glasses and brings her two inches from his nose to see her better. He feels for her heart, then shakes his head. He holds her in his left hand and pushes her tiny chest with his thumb, again and again.

Nothing happens.

He brings his mouth to her muzzle and breathes air into her lungs.

"Come on, baby, you can do this," he mumbles.

Standing there watching him squeeze her tiny body and blow life into her is the hardest thing I've ever done. My heart tells me that I should take her and care for her, but I know that Jones can do better with his opposable thumbs, so I force myself to stay put and watch.

He breathes air into her again and again until sweat drips

off the tip of his nose. His smell of despair is so bad it chokes me, but he keeps going.

It feels like a lifetime.

Then her chest starts moving. Her tongue pinks up, and she squeaks.

Jones sighs and wipes his forehead.

"There you go, Maddie. All yours."

I lick her clean, making sure I don't miss a spot. I clean her eyes and ears, though it's gonna be weeks until she needs them. I lick her tiny paws, thin as matchsticks, ending in sharp claws; her bald, soft belly; and her diminutive tail. She wiggles and squeaks in protest, but I won't stop until she barks the silliest little bark, telling me to leave her alone. Only then do I grab her by the scruff of her neck and drop her with the others.

I curl around them, exhausted and proud, and watch them crawl to the milk spouts — all of them, even the last.

I sigh with relief. Jones does too.

"Wow. Good job, Maddie. This last little one gave us a run for our money."

He gets the last collar.

"We'll call her Red. The runt of the litter."

3

———

FOUR WEEKS OLD

Even the most brilliant humans have a hard time understanding dogs, and I can tell you why. It's their upbringing.

Their moms didn't teach them to smell each other's butts so they could read each other's thoughts. They get trained to talk with their tongues instead, which only leads to miscommunication. That makes me wonder. How on earth did they get to dominate the world? It surely can't be their smarts. If I had to guess, I'd say it's their opposable thumbs that allow them to hold, click, and type. Boy, I wish I had a couple of those. Or at least a sniffing tablet.

Even Jones, who's as sharp as humans get, after the five years I've spent training him, doesn't get it. After he brought my Red back to life, he handed her to me without even sniffing her butt. I only took one whiff, and I knew Jones was wrong. He called her the runt of the litter, but she smelled like a champion. I knew right then that if any of my puppies got to change the world, it would be Red. She was deaf and blind and so weak she could barely latch, but I knew she'd go far.

But boy, what a pain in the butt!

I started homeschooling them when they were two weeks old. Not much you can teach them before that because they're born blind. Their eyes don't open for a couple weeks. They don't hear much either, with those round hamster ears. And they don't even know how to poop. I have to coax them into it, then clean them up.

The only things they can do are smell and yell. They'd find the milk bar if I took it down the street. No matter where I go, they crawl after me, screaming to high heaven. I don't have a quiet moment, even though they do nothing else but eat and sleep.

You'd think it would get easier as they grow older, but you'd be wrong. After two weeks, they open their eyes, and their ears start working. They get louder and louder and yelp like banshees whenever something doesn't go their way. Their personalities start showing too. You know that old saying: You can take the shepherd out of the farm, but you can't take the farm out of the shepherd? They don't yet know nothing about nothing, but they already know to get in the way.

Another week or two, and they'll be strong enough to go where they shouldn't and smart enough to get in trouble. Sticking your nose in power outlets, anyone? Sniffing out the cat, lapping the windshield washer, or wandering into the road? Take your pick.

A dog mom gets no rest. Not with these seven monsters competing for my attention. But I'm old enough to know the rules. It's easy since there are only two:

1. Keep them alive.

2.Teach them.

But they don't all learn the same.

Blue, #1, is the largest. He's black and tan, with a big blocky head, just like Rocky, his father. He's a good kid, my Blue, but not a fast learner. I need to teach him the same thing over and over. I wonder if it's his ears. The bigger the pup, the longer it takes their ears to perk up, and Blue's ears flop like a Labrador's.

Green, #2, is a big girl. She's a nice light tan with a black saddle who never barks back. She's the easiest to get along with.

Brown, #3, is always up for a nap unless he smells food.

White, #4, is the shy one. She loves playing and learning new things, but she'd never go explore on her own.

Black, #5, is jet-black and sleek. With his burning amber eyes and shiny coat, he's as handsome as they get. But what a contrarian! And he's stubborn as a mule.

Yellow, #6, is a lovely pup. Always happy but easily distracted. A gust of wind and she's off chasing some leaf, so I have a hard time making her focus on the things that matter.

Who's hardest to teach? Why Red, of course. She looks like a little dog angel, with her shiny black coat and golden eyebrows, but she's a pain in my butt every moment she's awake. She sneaks where the others never do and asks me questions I can't answer. She never tires of challenging the others, even Blue, who's twice as big as her. Thank Dog, he never gets mad, even when he should. Red's the kind of pup who can't leave any bush unsniffed and any leaf unturned.

Just yesterday, she snarked at Brown. "Why can't you squat like we do? Why lift your leg to the mailbox? How does that help? You never get mail anyhow."

I'd have fewer white hairs around my old muzzle if it weren't for Red. Fewer laughs, too. But I digress.

By week four, they're all up and about. Gone are the days I could leave them snoozing in their box to steal a quick nap in the library. They've learned to crawl out and sniff to track me. Well, not me, the milk bar, but it's the same since it's attached to me.

They're learning to get along. Or not. They recognize one another by the smell, and I can tell who likes who by the tail wags. Green and Blue stick together like glue. But Red growls and Black barks every time they catch a sniff of each other.

Good thing they all like Jones. They go nuts, wagging their little tails a mile a minute when he brings their puppy gruel. I don't know if it's his charming personality or the food, but I don't care. I'm delighted when he takes over so I can catch a break from their shark puppy teeth.

But I can't be gone long. So much to teach, so little time.

What's the first thing I taught them, you ask? The first thing I taught them was NO.

Of course, I can't say it, but there are other ways to talk than with your tongue. To send the message, I bare my teeth. If that doesn't do it, I growl. If that still doesn't cut it, I grab them by the scruff of their neck and drop them back in the box so they can start over.

Learning "NO" is essential. There's a world of dangers out there for a kid, canine or human: sharp things, hot stoves, fast cars, nasty old coots of many breeds. You need to teach your kids to stay away from danger.

They all learn differently, of course. Blue repeats the same mistake over and over. Yellow forgets what we're talking about. Brown is easy if you get him to wake up. But Red...

There's no end to how that pup can get in trouble. She's got to exhaust every single way to get in trouble with one thing before moving on to the next. She ate a bar of Dove Rose soap, Jones's boots, the fridge cable, and a corner of the sofa until she realized that some things were not food.

"Why do you always have to learn the hard way, Red?"

She looks at me with her round eyes, the color of a stormy sky.

"What do you mean, Mom? Is there any other way?"

Not for her, apparently. And for the first time in my six years, I wondered if parenthood was the right choice for me. Being a war dog may have been easier.

4

———

SIX WEEKS OLD

If I thought four weeks was bad, six weeks is worse.

The good news: the puppies have learned not to poop in their bed. The bad news: They poop everywhere else. More bad news: Their puppy shark teeth are so sharp I don't want them near my belly, so I spend half my time running away from them. But they've learned to run, so they chase me. Thank Dog, they can't yet climb on the sofa.

They've also learned to bite and fight.

Everything they see is a call to sniff, taste, and explore, from the Roomba to the cat. I don't much like the Roomba, but the cat is far more dangerous. Whiskey and I took forever to reach a precarious truce where I act like he doesn't exist while he glares at me from the window and hisses threats behind my back. Not good enough for you? Try his claws, and you'll understand.

Whiskey was already old and grumpy when I moved in with Jones five years ago. I was still a silly pup and needed a friend, so I jumped on him to play. But before you could say

"Milk Bone," he'd fluffed up like a toilet brush and hissed like a hairdryer.

I don't know about you, but I hate hairdryers. They burn your ears, mess up your hair, and hiss. Better avoid them, even though they don't have claws. As for Whiskey? That one's better lost than found.

But the kids don't know it, so they keep chasing him. Fortunately, they've learned "NO" by now, so they let him be when I'm around. But when I'm not watching...oh well, I guess they're old enough to handle his lessons. I just hope it won't cost them an eye.

The sky's blue and the sun is shining as I homeschool my Magnificent Seven in the front yard under the blooming maples. I'd love to take them on a field trip, but I need to hustle. I only have a few weeks to teach them all they need to know before they leave for their forever homes to look after their humans. And, after five litters, I've got a lesson plan to cover the basics, but I take questions as they arise. Today's subject is meeting new dogs.

"Some of your humans may already have pets who are prone to thinking that those humans belong to them. They're wrong, of course. We are German shepherds; therefore, everyone under our roof belongs to us. We must protect them at any cost."

Yellow raises her paw.

"Yes?"

"What if they have a cat and a kid, and the cat scratches the kid? Do we kill the cat?"

I choke.

"Well, now. That's a bit extreme. First, we growl. That should warn the cat and intimidate him into withdrawing. If he refuses, we bark for help. If no help is available, we can attempt to reposition the cat by dragging him away. But only ever do that as a last resort. I can't remember any situation where attacking a cat turned out to be a good idea. Now, if you're only dealing with armed robbers, that should be fine. You all should be able to handle that."

"Mom?"

"Yes, Red."

"How about we reposition the kid instead of the cat?"

Why didn't I think of that?

"Repositioning the kid is a great idea. Safer too. Their claws are usually clipped. Just drag it away."

"Mom?"

"Yes, Green?"

"What if the other dogs don't like us?"

"Sadly, that often happens. The other dogs are used to controlling their resources: The food, the sofa, the humans' affection — they won't like sharing any of that. That's when you have to act like a victim. You're all small and cute. Let the other dog growl, show his teeth, and maybe even bite you a little while your human is watching. That should oust them. But don't attack them; otherwise, people may blame you. Stupid, I know, but most humans aren't known for being smart. That's why they need us. Everyone all set with meeting new dogs?"

Red cocks her head. With her right ear standing and the left one flopped over, she's cute as can be. But what a rascal!

"Mom, how was it when you met Father?"

Like I said. What does that have to do with anything?

I glare at her, but she won't relent.

"We talked about meeting new dogs. Father's a dog, too, isn't he?"

I guess we're about to have The Talk. I hadn't planned it for today, but that's Red for you. Always comes in from left field.

"Your father, Rocky, is more than a dog; he's a hero. He fought in Afghanistan as an explosive-detecting K-9. Then he got wounded on a mission and received a Purple Heart."

"Is that a treat?"

"No. It's a dog tag. That lets everyone know that Rocky is a hero."

"Was he wearing it when you met him? Is that why you fell in love with him?"

Oh boy.

"Our... mating was arranged. Jones wanted us to have puppies, so he looked for a stud with a great pedigree. That's how he found your father. We went to meet him when the time was right."

"How did you know that the time was right?"

"I was...feeling very hot."

"And then?"

"We drove to Rocky's home. We met and sniffed each other's butts to introduce each other. That's how I found out that he was interested in me."

"Were you interested in him too?"

"Very much."

"And then?"

"We spent some time together, and then Jones and I drove home."

"Was he handsome?'

"Very."

"Was he romantic?"

"He was...sexy."

"And then?"

"Then I had you."

"You miss him?"

"Not yet."

The girls' eyes shine as they hope to meet their Dog Charming someday, and I don't have the heart to tell them that dog love isn't all that it's cracked up to be. What Rocky and I had was a one-time stand rather than romance, but that's how I got these seven darlings, and I wouldn't trade them for the world.

5

EIGHT WEEKS OLD

Summer's almost here. The maple leaves got so thick they turn light green, block the hot sun, and keep the ground smelling like mushrooms. I love the soft mud embracing my paws, the gentle breeze tickling my ears, and even the sparrows quarreling above, even though they distract Yellow. But she's a big girl now, and she does her best to ignore them as she lines up for today's lesson with the others.

I sniff to inspect them one by one: Blue sitting up proudly, his left ear almost up. Green, her eyes glued to me, eager to please. Black, twitching his tail impatiently. Brown, his eyes half closed. White, her ears perked up, listening for any danger. Yellow, who's ready to leap after a fuzzy caterpillar. And Red.

They're almost ready, and I don't know if I'm more proud or brokenhearted. Any day now, their new humans will come to take them home, and I can't imagine what Jones and I will do all alone!

But for now, I struggle to cram every bit of canine knowledge into their thirsty brains. They've already learned to smell each other's thoughts and know they should offer their butts to their betters for sniffing. And, since they're just pups, everyone is their better, from babies to cats, let alone whatever mangy mutt their human collected from some shelter.

But that won't last long. Give my pups a few months, and they'll run their households with an iron paw.

I put my last touches on their education: Be polite. Be honest. Be paranoid. That's the only way you'll be ready for bad things before they happen. Humans think being paranoid is terrible, but they're wrong. If I don't watch the mailman every day, how will I know when it's not the mailman but some Ninja assassin? If I don't smell my food before I eat it, how will I know what's in it? If I don't sniff Jones's privates every morning, how will I ever know if he's still male? Humans say: Trust but verify. How silly is that? I say: sniff, recheck, then trust.

I check them one by one. They're all clean and proper, and they smell ready. I wag my tail in approval and ask, "What's our motto?"

They lift their muzzles and bark like one.

"Utility and intelligence."

"Good."

"Mom?"

"Yes, Red."

"Why is this our motto?"

"Because we, German shepherds, are useful and bright."

"But we're beautiful too!"

"Sure we are, but beauty is secondary. A dog lacking the intelligence, temperament, and physical prowess to do his duty is worthless, and therefore not a German shepherd. That's what Captain Max Von Stephanitz said."

"Mom?"

"Yes, Red?"

"Who's that?"

"The human who developed our breed. But that's not important right now. Where was I?"

"Mom?"

"Yes, Red?"

"How do you know what humans say?"

"I don't. Not really. But humans seldom have anything interesting to say. They have a few good words, like 'ball,' 'treat,' and 'walk.' But most of the time, they just spew gibberish to each other. Sometimes even lies. A great French philosopher — I think he was a poodle — once said that speech was given to humans to disguise their thoughts. He was right. Poodles are almost as smart as us, though they look ridiculous. I guess they can't help it, being French and all. Still, never forget that words are worse than useless — they're deceiving. The one thing that matters is what humans think."

"And how do you know that?

"Smell them, dear. Thoughts, feelings, and emotions release scents that we dogs can read just like Jones reads his books. Sniff them, and you'll know if they're happy, lonely, or in heat. Or lying. It's that easy."

"Does that work with other things or just people?"

"It works with every living thing but plants. Plants are weird. They have their own agenda, and they'll lie to you just like humans lie to each other. Take garlic, for example. Its smell says: Don't touch me; I'm evil. But if you ever try Bolognese... or garlic roasted lamb. Mmm. Plants lie to keep from getting eaten. Of course, some lie the other way, like hickory and maple, who pretend to be bacon. Phew! Liars. But, other than plants, everybody smells like they are."

"How do you know which is which? Like who to trust, and who not to?"

This is the question, isn't it? I could debate that for hours, but the others are no longer paying attention. And I know that no matter what I tell her, she must still learn the hard way.

I lick her nose and sigh.

"Go sniff Whiskey. But don't get too close. Then come back and tell me what you learned."

6

WHISKEY

Her head held high, her silly left ear flopping with every step, Red leaves on her mission, and I curl in the shade to watch the kids chase each other. I remember the day I met Whiskey.

I'd just arrived from a long, long trip. I'm an immigrant, you see. I was born in Berlin. My mother was said to come from pure Alsatian bloodlines going back to Blondie, Hitler's favorite German shepherd. Some say he loved Blondie so much that he killed her to make sure the Russians didn't catch and torture her. Others say he only tried his cyanide pill on her to ensure it worked.

Either way, Hitler killed Blondie and asked her handler to kill her five young pups, but the man kept one.

Wolf was just weeks old, but she was worth her weight in gold. Mother said she was our great-grandmother, but I don't know. I think it was just the breeder's marketing ploy. Regardless, Mother was the jewel of our kennel, and her puppies were in great demand.

My father, Admiral Von Tirpitz, was a well-known Schutzhund champion who swore to die protecting his humans. I've never met him, but I often heard our breeder brag about him.

"Tell me about Father," I asked Mother.

She sighed.

"He's very handsome. He's dark and strong, with hardly any color but his eyebrows, and he's got the best-looking tail I've ever seen. You take after him, Maddie."

Sadly, my tail is the only way I took after Father. All my brothers and even my sister Eva had already started their Schutzhund training. Not me. I love food and naps, and I hate fights. I'd trade all the wars in the world for a mouth-watering pepperoni pizza with anchovies and capers. I'd even sell them for a hot dog.

I hung my head.

"Mother, I'm sorry if I'm not who you want me to be."

Mother slapped her tail to the ground in a dog smile.

"Are you kidding? Don't worry, Schatzi, I'm not into fighting either; otherwise, I wouldn't be here breeding. I'll take the food, the love, and the good life. Thank Dog, we aren't all like your father."

Mother loved Riesling grapes, Wiener schnitzel, and telling stories, and I loved listening to her. We had a great life until the day they came to get me.

I cocked my head in surprise.

"You must be mistaken. I don't think anyone wants me."

The man checked his papers, then my collar.

"You are Madeleine Rose Kahn, yes? You're going to America."

I froze.

"America? Are you sure? I don't know anyone there."

He shrugged, locked me in a crate, and shipped me to New York.

The journey was long and scary, and all I had to help me through it were Mother's words.

"But Mother, how will I manage there? I can't even speak their language."

She licked my nose.

"You'll learn, Schatzi. Dogs are dogs, and people are people no matter where you go. You'll just be your usual sweet self, and they'll love you. I know they will. And America's not that bad. Your aunt Elsie was there for a Shutzhund contest, and she said they have something called bacon that tastes even better than schnitzel. Burgers too. And just think how much worse it could be. You could go to India, where they're all vegetarian; to Kuwait, where they don't eat pork, not even Schweinshaxe; or to England, where they overcook their food."

I hoped she was right, but I was scared stiff. And aunt Elsie, who'd been everywhere and knew everything, had told me about someplace where they ate dogs, especially black ones, so I was worried they might eat me.

But by the time I arrived, I was too exhausted to care. Go ahead, eat me. Put me out of my misery, I thought.

The man who opened my crate didn't smell hungry. He was blue-eyed and chunky, with round glasses and a scanty beard, and he smelled like Dove soap.

"Welcome home, Maddie," he said and scratched my ears.

I lifted my muzzle, hoping he'd lick my nose. I was so

lonely and sad that I needed a pick-me-up. He didn't, but he fed me.

Kibble. Phew!

I tried to stay positive. It could be worse, I thought. I could be going to war.

That's when I sniffed Whiskey. Old coot!

I'm about to settle for a nap when Red blasts through the doggy door, her muzzle covered in scratches. Her tiny hackles are up, and her eyes are hot with anger, but, thank Dog, she still has two.

I want to lick her and make it better, but I can't. She needs to learn something, and it's not that mom will kiss away the pain.

"What happened?"

"That old dumbass scratched the bejesus out of me!"

"Watch it, young lady. Why?"

"I tried to smell his butt, but he got frantic when I lifted his tail. I tried to explain that I was just sniffing his feelings, but he plumped up and hissed, then started screeching like a police car. No matter how I tried, I couldn't turn him around to smell his butt."

"So, what did you learn?"

"That he's a creep?"

"Anything else?"

"Cats don't play by the rules."

Now we're talking.

"Which rules?"

"Dogs' rules."

"They surely don't. Anything else?"

"That misunderstandings can hurt you?"

Not bad for an eight-week-old pup. I lick her wounds and

get her settled with the others, then lick my paws as I watch them snore and think about their future. Red is the smallest and the fiercest. That may be good someday, but for now, it's nothing but trouble. People want submissive dogs, even if that's not what they need. Humans need someone to take over and make decisions, and my Red is just the one to do it. But they're not smart enough to know it.

7

THE STUD

The day I dreaded is here. A dozen humans have come to check out my puppies, and I watch them like a hawk. They ooh and aah over them, and that's bittersweet. I'm proud I'm their mom, and I'm glad the humans can see how special they are, but I'm terrified to let my kids leave with these strangers. I'll probably never see them again, and the thought of allowing my pups to go through life without me breaks my heart.

Fortunately, I don't have time to feel sorry for myself. I must watch them and ensure they each choose the right home for them. Otherwise, they won't be happy, and neither will their new humans. The right match is of utmost importance.

Blue is the most popular. He's big and handsome, and humans love that. I don't understand why humans love to brag about the size of stuff: their dogs, their cars, and their homes. Everything but their wives. They think bigger is better, but it's not. Better is better. And my pups are the best.

The visitors watch the kids, then ask for one-on-ones with those they like the most. Fortunately, the kids know what to do. I taught them well.

"If you want a good life, choose the humans that smell like food. You may eat bacon, pizza, and even grapes. And a job is no longer a job when you love it."

There's more to life than just food, of course, but the kids are too young to understand. And that's what Jones and I are here for.

I'm sniffing an old couple to see who's the best match for them when a familiar scent tickles my nose. I turn around, and it's Rocky. I hadn't seen him since our only date, and I didn't miss him, but his scent stirred something inside me.

He wags his tail and offers me his butt. He smells solid and confident, just like he did then. He turns to lick my nose, and my heart softens.

"Hi, Maddie."

"Hi, Rocky."

"It's so good to see you. You look hotter than ever."

He's right. It's a hot day, and after running from one interview to another, I'm so hot that my tongue hangs to my knees. But the wag of his tail and the sparkle in his eyes tells me he meant it as a compliment.

"Same here."

"I'm here with my hooman. I brought him to choose a pup. You know the deal – the pick of the litter goes to the stud."

"Of course."

"You did a great job, Maddie. They're all beautiful."

"Sure they are. How can they not be when they're yours?"

Rocky cocks his head and raises his brown eyebrows,

wondering if I'm kidding. Just in case you didn't know: being a stud is not about the brain.

"Which one should I get?"

"What are you looking for in a pup?'

"A strong, handsome male to keep the bloodline alive."

"Which one do you like?"

He watches them play in the grass. Blue has pinned down Brown, who's about to fall asleep. Green chases Yellow, who stole her ball. White watches a fly as Black and Red have a showdown over a pinecone.

"That Blue is handsome."

"He sure is."

"Green looks good, too, even though she's a girl."

I snort.

Rocky turns his eyes to Red. She's still the smallest. Her hackles up, she bares her teeth and growls the funniest little growl. It looks awful cute, but Black knows better. He backs away from her pinecone like he doesn't even care. Red raises her funny eyebrows and watches him leave, and I can't believe how much she's Rocky's spitting image.

"That little one."

"Yes."

"She's something else. Why is she so small?"

"She's the runt of the litter."

"Oh."

He loses interest and turns to sniff my tail, then licks my nose again.

"See you soon, baby. It's been lonely without you."

Poppycock. I smelled not one, not two, but three females he met just last week. But there's no point in mentioning it, so I just wag my tail.

"Sure. Did you make a choice?"

"I did. I'll have to run that by my hooman, but I think Blue is the right choice for us."

"I agree. That's who I'd choose if I were you."

"Thanks, sweetheart. See you soon, OK?"

He gives me a last lusty glance and saunters away to the crowd's delight. They're here to see him, too. Our little breeder business promised the humans they could see both parents when they got a pup, and the humans loved it. That's how they know what to expect when the kids grow up.

Rocky prances away like the dork he is, but he's right. Blue is more like him than any of the others, even though Red looks just like him. But in dogs, like in people, it's not about the looks. It's about the heart. As a famous Wheaten terrier once barked, "It's not the size of the dog in the fight; it's the size of the fight in the dog." And nobody has more fight in them than Red, not even Rocky. He's just not smart enough to see it.

8

CHOOSING NEW HOMES

After Rocky took Blue, the others went like hotcakes. I got dizzy sprinting from one pup to the other, making sure that each of my babies chose the right home for them. You think that's easy? Think again. My puppies were all well-bred and lovely, but they all needed different homes to thrive and give their best. Matching each of them with the right home was essential.

Sadly, humans don't know what they need. An elderly couple with an evident love for food and antipathy to exercise was interested in Red. Thank Dog that Jones nipped that in the bud. I've trained him for years, so he knows that someone like Red needs lots of action. And if she can't find it, she'll make it happen. He matched them with Brown, whose life goal is to be a couch potato.

White adopted a female who smelled sad and lonely. She needed someone to spoil and cherish, and White was the perfect match. Yellow got a family with three young kids who are just as wild as her. I bet they'll be active enough to keep her on her paws.

After much sniffing and thinking, Green decided on an elderly couple. They smelled loving, but they needed lots of help. Judging by the smell of his pajamas, the male was friendly but forgetful, and his female had her work cut out caring for him. My Green will look after them both, and they'll love her to bits.

But believe it or not, two kids didn't find their forever homes. Black and Red are still here, and neither Jones nor I are surprised.

After I put them to sleep, Jones opened a beer. He settled in his recliner but didn't open his book. He scratched his head and looked at me instead.

"What are we going to do with those two, Maddie? They're lovely pups, but they don't fit the mold."

I cocked my head.

"Can we keep them here?"

"I'm sorry, baby, we can't afford it. My teacher's pension isn't enough. The vet bills alone would make us broke. The pups need to go. But where?"

I wish we could keep them, but I know Jones is right. Even more, the kids need to find their calling and live their lives. They can't retire before they even start.

"You know, Maddie, Black may be a bit strongheaded for a pet, but he'd make a great working dog. And he's so hand-some, he could be a stud. With that pedigree and good looks, he could entertain the ladies for years. Wouldn't that be a great life?"

I chortle. Like Jones knows anything about ladies! I've been here for five years without seeing any females visit. But he has a point. Black is bright and as handsome as they get, and he's got the fire to pass on to his kids.

"How about Red?"

Jones shakes his head.

"I don't know, Maddie. I love her with all my heart, but I've never had a dog like her. I don't know what to do."

I sigh.

"I do. Red is just like my brothers and sisters. The Schutzhund gene skipped me, but it found Red. She's got the heart of a working dog. She needs a mission."

Jones sighed. "I'll see what I can do."

That whole night I didn't catch a wink. I watched my pups snore and dream about running in the fields, feeling like a criminal. Who'd send their baby to a life of work instead of leisure? But Red had scoffed at every chance to be a pet. And she had to find her place in the world.

I was glad when Jones found Black a breeding program. I knew he'd have a good life. And I secretly hoped that Jones might relent and decide to keep Red. For a while, it looked like that could happen.

So I taught her everything I knew, hoping it may come in handy someday. I'm no longer young, and I hoped Red would look after Jones when I'm gone.

But that wasn't to be.

Two uniformed humans came to see Red. I knew she was going to war, and my heart broke. How will my baby manage all alone?

But when they tried to order her around, she stood up to them and made me proud. My Red may be just a pup, but I know she's destined for greatness. I bet she'll show the army a thing or two. When I licked her goodbye, I hoped it wouldn't be forever.

My heart broke as I watched the jeep take her away. Jones wiped his eyes with his old red sweater that Red had eaten a hole in, and we walked back inside, wondering what to do with ourselves. The house was just as empty as our hearts.

I curled by the fireplace with my nose under my tail to catch a nap, like I always do when I'm sad. Jones turned on the TV to a war movie, but he gave up.

"I can't watch this, Maddie. I'm so sorry Red had to go."

He smelled guilty as sin, and I knew he was thinking that, maybe, if he stopped buying books and drinking beer, he could have kept us both.

But Red wouldn't be happy. She needs to go places, do things, and meet people. Her life hasn't even started, while ours are almost over.

I licked his hand.

"That's OK, Jones. You did what you had to do. She wouldn't be happy if she stayed. And neither would we."

9

THE FAILED MATING

After the pups all left, Jones and I tried to settle back into our old life. We took long walks; I lay by the fire watching Jones read; we watched old movies and munched on popcorn. But the popcorn tasted like cardboard, and Jones sat staring at his book, forgetting to turn the pages. Our life smelled sad and lonely, and we had no future. It was like we were just waiting to die.

But one morning Jones checked his email, humphed, and glanced at me over his glasses.

"Hey, Maddie. I got an email about Rocky. They're asking for a date. What do you think?"

I cocked my head to think. A date? With Rocky? I don't know. I don't know if I'm ready for another litter, now or ever. I don't feel sexy.

But we're so lonely...

Jones understood.

"You're six, sweetheart. This may be your last chance. You want to give it a try?"

I wish I knew. I have mixed feelings about Rocky. He's handsome and makes great children, but his wits? I've seen brighter squirrels squished in the road. And the way he talks about girls...

But we're so lonely...It would be lovely to have a houseful of puppies to love, chase, and teach. One last time.

I wagged my tail.

"OK. Let's give it a try."

A few days later, Jones brushed me until I shone, clipped my nails, and did his best to make me pretty. He would have sprayed me with Febreze if I didn't bare my teeth and growl.

"Come on, Jones. I've just rolled in a dead fish, for Dog's sake. Do you think you can make me smell any better?"

Rocky agreed. He sniffed me, and his tail quivered in excitement.

"Maddie! How good to see you! I've been waiting for you forever!"

He was lying, of course — I could smell his last two females from the door. But he was intent on being charming.

"What a great litter we made last time! Blue's new humans rave about him. Same with Black. His folks couldn't be more pleased. Our pups are top-of-the-line. But let's have more males this time, shall we? Nobody wants females."

My hackles went up.

"Seriously? What's wrong with females?"

"Nothing, really, but males are where it's at. They keep the bloodline alive, bring the energy and fight the wars. Females are just there for breeding."

My blood rushed to my head. I got so mad my eyes crossed.

"Really? Without females, who'd continue the line? And some females fight wars. Remember Red?"

Rocky cocked his head.

"Red? That little thing with brown eyebrows?"

"Yes. Your daughter Red. She went to war. Unlike you. You're doing nothing but breeding."

Rocky flattened his ears.

"Come on, Maddie. I was just kidding. Or something."

He stepped closer to sniff my butt, but I pulled away so fast he couldn't get a whiff. I bared my fangs and growled like a Harley Davidson blowing through a red light.

"Don't touch me, Buster."

Rocky tucked his tail between his legs and stepped back.

"Come on, Maddie! You've got to be kidding! After all the good times we've had?"

"That was then, and this is now. You're nothing but an egotistical, dim-witted stud. I don't want to see you again. You're like last winter's snow. Gone."

Jones and I drove home in silence.

"I guess there'll be no more puppies for us, eh?"

I felt guilty. I knew Jones looked forward to another litter to give us hope and make us feel alive. And help the bottom line. But I couldn't do it.

"Sorry, Jones."

He scratched my ears.

"It's OK, Maddie. We may both be too old for another challenge."

I don't know. I don't know if I'm too old for another challenge, but I'm too old to put up with Rocky's crap.

10

———

A HOPELESS WINTER

Who knew that when you give up on your future plans, you also give up on your future? After the Rocky fiasco, our hopes flew away with the leaves.

The sun made itself scarce, and the days shrank and faded. Even our walks became a chore. By the time the freezing November drizzle gave way to sleet and slush, we only waited to die.

We even stopped watching movies and gave up on the popcorn. We just sat by the fire to chat about the good old days when the kids kept us busy.

"Remember when Whiskey chased White, and she hid in the vent?"

"And that time Yellow ate a peach pit and couldn't poop for days? I thought she'd need surgery."

"And when Red ate your boot and puked it all over the kitchen floor?"

I'd always loved winter, but this one was hard to love. So I started looking forward to spring, hoping the sun would melt away the gloom. But it was a long wait.

Then Jones fell, and spring became too far.

We'd gone to get the mail, though I never got any. But that gave us an excuse to get out, stretch our legs, and check on the world. I was just sniffing the peemail when someone screamed. I turned around. Jones had slipped and fallen on the ice.

I tried to help him, but I couldn't get him to his feet, no matter how hard I tried.

I dragged him back to the house, but I couldn't pull him up the steps. He's a good man, Jones, but not a small one. I needed help.

"Wait here," I barked, running down the street to seek help. Nobody.

I ran from door to door, barking like an army of cats were invading, until an old blue van turned the corner. They tried to avoid me, but I got in their way and barked and barked until they stopped.

The driver lowered the window.

"What's up, pup?"

"I need help, please. My human fell, and I can't get him up," I barked.

When the ambulance came, they loaded Jones onto a stretcher and took him. I tried to follow, but they wouldn't let me.

"That's OK, Maddie. You stay and take care of our home. I'll be back," Jones said.

The men locked me in. I rushed to the dining room window to see them leave, my heart full of worry. They were taking Jones away when he was hurt and needed me more than ever. I barked and barked, but they didn't stop. So I ran to the door and scratched it to get out, but it was locked.

I ran back to the window, but they were gone.

So I sat by the window to wait.

I waited and waited, but they didn't come back.

It got dark, then light again.

Jones didn't return.

So I kept waiting.

It got dark again.

Still nothing.

I got so hungry I left the window for a moment. I went to the kitchen to look for something to eat, and I'd almost finished the dish sponge when I heard the key. Jones was back!

I rushed to greet him.

"I'm so glad you're back! I missed you terribly! I'm sorry about the mess in the dining room, but the doggy door was locked."

The door opened, and a woman came in. She measured me with cold eyes and took off her fur coat.

"You must be Maddie."

I wagged my tail.

"Yes."

I sniffed her. She smelled like cats.

"I'm Gwen, Jones's daughter. He broke his hip and needs surgery. He asked me to take care of you. He won't be back."

I cocked my head.

"He won't be back? You mean today?"

Gwen hung up her coat.

"After surgery, he'll go to rehab, and then I'll find him a nursing home. He can't live alone anymore."

I struggled to understand.

"What do you mean, live alone? I'm right here!"

She shrugged and walked from room to room to check them out. She shook her head at Jones' overstuffed bookshelves and gagged at the mess in the dining room.

I knew I should feel guilty, but I didn't. I don't care what she thinks. The only human I care about is Jones.

He won't be back, she said. But she's wrong. Jones would never leave me like I'd never leave him.

Or would he?

11

THE SHELTER

The next few days were a blur. I got dizzy running from the dining room window, where I watched for Jones's return, to following Gwen who packed Jones's clothes, threw away his books, and made call after call about me.

Her phone voice was sweet as honey, but her eyes were cold steel as they measured me.

"Thank you for taking my call. I'm calling about a dog that needs a home. Her owner is moving into a nursing home and can't take her with him. How old? She's almost seven, a pure-bred German shepherd. Is she good with cats? I don't know. I don't know about kids, either. She's been with no cats and no kids here. No dogs either. She'd probably do best in a house with no kids or pets."

Gwen sighed and sat her phone on the coffee table.

"Bad news, Maddie. Nobody wants an old dog. It looks like you're going to the shelter."

I cocked my head. I didn't understand. I didn't know what a shelter was and didn't care. All I cared about was Jones.

"But what will Jones do? Who'll take care of him?"

Gwen snickered.

"He'll have people, qualified people, to look after him. And they don't allow dogs. Not even cats, for God's sake."

Gwen slammed the door behind her, and I spent the night wondering how to find Jones. I didn't care what she said; I knew he needed me. Nobody knew him like I do. I knew when he was happy, and I knew when he was sad. I knew when he got excited about something he read and needed to explain it to me so he could understand it better, and when he felt lonely and needed my head in his lap.

Whatever Gwen said was hogwash. I knew that Jones would come back as soon as he could, but what if she put me in a shelter, whatever that was, and he couldn't find me? I had to do something. But what?

I was so tired and broken I couldn't think of anything, and by the time Gwen loaded me in her car, it was too late.

"Where are we going?"

"The County Shelter. That's where people drop the dogs and cats they no longer want."

My jaw dropped. I didn't know such a thing existed. How can a human not want his dog? That's like not wanting your heart. Or your tail. They're part of you. How can you throw them away?

She's got to be lying, I thought. But I was wrong.

The shelter was a long ugly building lined with kennels packed with dogs of every shape, breed, and color.

The stench of sadness and despair hit my nose, and I pulled back. But Gwen would have none of it. She handed my leash to the kid at the door and left before I got to ask about

Jones. So I tried to follow her, but the kid pulled me back, and the door slammed shut.

"Hey Gwen, where's Jones? How can I find him?" I barked.

She didn't answer. But a hundred dogs started barking.

The kid dragged me into the long concrete prison, and all hell broke loose. The barks and the howls shook the walls. A hundred inmates stuck their muzzles through the wires to sniff me, heckle me, and cheer me on.

"Hello, baby. Sprechen Sie Deutch?" yapped a rat-like chihuahua, showing his yellow crooked teeth.

"Look at the sexy tail on that bitch," a spotted Great Dane muttered.

"A German shepherd? Here in the shelter? Are you for real?" growled a curly black mutt.

I did my best to ignore them, but it wasn't easy. I'd never been treated with such indignity. And it got even worse when the kid locked me in a kennel and left.

I sniffed every inch of my new quarters, but all I got was the burning smell of bleach and the stench of the other inmates' overwhelming sadness. My heart choking with sorrow, I curled in the straw, wishing I was home in my memory foam bed. I lay my nose on my paws and covered it with my tail, pretending to sleep.

The hecklers finally settled and returned to lapping their water, scratching their fleas, and licking their privates. All but a roguishly handsome golden retriever three cells down. He stared at me, wagging his tail like he knew me. I tried to ignore him, but he was polite. And persistent.

"What's your name, beautiful lady?"

"I'm Madeline Rose Kahn Van Jones. You?"

"I'm Ranger."

His gravelly bark made me warm inside.

"Ranger? That's it?"

"Yep. That's because I never stick around for too long. But let's talk about you. How did someone like you end up in a place like this?"

"It's a long story."

"We have nothing but time."

"My human fell. They took him to the hospital and kept him there. Then his daughter took over, and she brought me here. How about you?"

"I needed a place to spend the winter, and this was just as good as any. There are a few sketchy characters, but then you meet someone special like you every once in a while, and it makes it all worth it."

I wagged my tail to fan myself.

"Thanks, I think. What happens next?"

"Not much. We hang out and sniff the breeze. Sometimes humans come to adopt someone. That's always a good day."

"What happens to those who don't get adopted?"

"They wait."

"What for?"

"To get adopted."

"And if they don't?"

"If they don't, they die. Have you ever heard about kill shelters?"

12

AN UNLIKELY HERO

"What's a kill shelter?"

"Just what you'd think. No-kill shelters only take in the dogs and cats they know they can find homes for. The others take everyone, no matter how old, sick, or damaged, and they try to find them a home. Sometimes they can, but sometimes they can't. When they run out of space, and they need to make room for the newcomers, they put to sleep the dogs nobody wants."

Wow!

That got me thinking. I know nobody wants me. I've heard Gwen trying to pawn me off to a bunch of people, but none of them wanted me. Nobody wants an old dog, she said. So this is the end of my journey.

Well then.

I lay my nose on my paws to think.

I've had it good.

I had six litters of beautiful puppies. I taught them how to look after their humans, urged them to make the world a better place, and sent them out into the world. I'd love to see them and find out how they're doing — Green with her old folks, Yellow with her wild kids, Brown with his couch potatoes, and Red with her soldiers. I'd love to know about my other litters too, and I miss them all, but I'm not worried. They're all, to the last one, proper German shepherds, eager to do their duty and living by our motto: Utility and intelligence. Wherever they are, I know they'll keep their humans safe and make them feel loved, and they'll look after every soul under their roofs, from goldfish to horses. Even cats. Because that's the kind of dogs they are.

The one I'm worried about is Jones, and thinking of him breaks my heart.

I failed him.

He didn't send me away. He got sick, and Gwen took over. She grabbed his home and ditched the things he loved. She hijacked his life, dispatched him to a nursing home, and then got rid of me to keep me from helping him.

I should have seen that coming.

The thought of Jones alone in a hospital somewhere, without anyone to pet, read to, or hug, without his books, movies, and popcorn, breaks my heart. Jones was my responsibility, and I failed him. I was a bad dog.

My ears flatten, and my tail tucks between my legs in shame. I'm heartbroken and overwhelmed. This is terrible. I must find a way to redeem myself. I have to get out of here and find Jones. But how?

"You OK, Maddie?" Ranger barks.

He smelled my distress from his cell twenty feet away. He knows that I'm worried, and he cares. My heart softens. He's the only one who likes me here. I don't know if it's my attitude or my German accent, but all the others yap behind my back.

Ranger smells my thoughts.

"Don't worry, Maddie. They're just envious. Every one of them would trade his coat for yours. You're purebred and beautiful. You won't end up chopped. Humans will fight over you."

I wag my tail to thank him, but I know better. I don't feel beautiful. I feel dirty, tired, and old. And I long for one of the baths Jones used to give me. I used to hate shampoo, especially the menthol one, but now I wish I hadn't been such a pain in the butt. The way I look, I'll be lucky if I don't get fleas.

"I need to get out of here, Ranger."

"Really? But why? This is better than living in the streets in winter. It's warm and dry, and we don't even have to steal to eat. The boys may be rough, but they're fun to watch. No cars to squish us or even honk at us. Nobody even throws stones. Why leave?"

"I need to find Jones. His daughter took him hostage, and I need to save him. He doesn't belong in a nursing home like I don't belong here. I need to get out and find him."

"I'm not gonna lie to you, baby; it won't be easy. You sure you wanna do this?"

"Absolutely."

"OK. Let me think."

It turns out that Ranger snores while he thinks. He slept the whole day, the entire night, and the day after. I wondered if he'd died, but he didn't smell like it.

Then he woke up, shook like he meant business, and barked.

"Hey, Maddie. You still wanna get out?"

"Absolutely."

"OK then. Tonight's tech is that pimpled kid who's always on his phone. He never closes the kennel door when he cleans the cells. Wait until he opens my crate, then start yelling like someone shot you. Roll on the ground and pretend you're dying. When he opens your door, dash out after me. I'll show you the way out."

"What if he cleans my crate first?"

"Then I'll do the squealing. But wait for me; otherwise, you won't get far."

I take in his ragged orange coat, the long scar marring his left cheek and that crooked tail that must have broken and healed wrong. There's no doubt that Ranger has had an exciting life, and he's no stranger to trouble. Does that make him a troublemaker or a survivor? Should I trust him and go with this silly plan?

His eyes shine with intelligence, and he smells confident and loyal, but I'm torn. I can't remember a single time when following a male turned out to be a good idea. But what else can I do?

"I'll be ready."

13

THE GREAT ESCAPE

This day drags like it will never end. I try to nap, but I'm too wired. So, to kill time, I watch the other inmates. I wonder if they have unfinished business outside and dream of escape. I tried to sniff their thoughts, but their feelings got in the way like feelings always do. My heart grew heavy with their fear, loneliness, and dejection.

I remember when Jones once read to me: "Happy people are all alike, but every unhappy person is unhappy in its own way," or something like that. I think he was talking about humans, but it's the same with dogs.

My misery is not like the other dogs'. Kill shelter or not, I don't feel scared or dejected. I'm guilty and angry. I'm guilty of having failed Jones and mad at myself for it. And, as always, anger trumps guilt. By the time the pimply kid comes to clean our cages, I've channeled all my shame into being angry with Gwen, and I'm shaking with rage.

The kid leaves the door open and starts cleaning the cells, just like Ranger said. His eyes are glued to the screen, and his earbuds are stuck in his ears. He's more into his phone than the mop he sloshes around, and I wonder why he's here if he doesn't care about us dogs. But I don't have much time to ponder. He opens my crate. Three cells down, Ranger yells like someone bit him.

His barks are loud enough to shake the walls, but the kid doesn't hear a thing. So I get in his face and bark like the mailman's coming.

"Seriously, dude! Get those freaking things out of your ears."

The kid startles and takes out his earbuds. He turns to see where the yelling comes from, and Ranger drops to the ground, pumping the air with his paws like he's about to die, and the whole kennel erupts in chaos.

"What the heck?"

The kid drops the mop and rushes to Ranger. He opens the door, and Ranger blasts out. He knocks down the kid and dashes down the hallway. I take off in hot pursuit, and before you can shake your tail, we're out the kennel door.

"Good job, everyone! This way, baby," Ranger barks.

We dash down the narrow hallway, then Ranger hooks a left to a small storage room half-full of straw bales, the kind they use for bedding. A wintery breeze smelling like freedom comes in through the window by the ceiling.

"That's the window they keep open for ventilation. Can you make it?" Ranger barks.

Oh, boy. I don't know. That's Dog awful high, and I can't remember the last time I had to run or jump. I'm terribly out of shape. But I'm on a mission, and I'm boiling with rage.

I claw my way to the top of the pile and leap to grab onto the window frame.

Not even close.

Somewhere behind, the kid calls for help.

I step back to take a running start. I plant my paws, leap on the highest bale, and claw my way up the concrete wall. Two more inches and...

I fall back.

The dogs bark, a phone rings, the kid shouts. Loud boots echo in the hallway.

They're getting close.

I look at the window. It's too far.

"Sorry, Ranger. I'm too old; I can't make it. You go."

Ranger growls.

"Are you kidding? I'm not going anywhere without you. Let's try this."

He squats under the window to give me a paw up. That's the most beautiful thing anyone has ever done for me. I'd love to lick his nose and thank him, but I don't have time. I dash from the door, climb the straw bales and plant my paws on Ranger's back. I grab the windowsill, claw my way up, and before you can say "Beggin' Strip," I'm flying out the window.

I hit the frozen ground headfirst.

Oops.

I get up and shake to get my bearings.

I'm out on a dark, empty side street. Nothing is moving but a long, twisted shadow. It wags its tail, and it turns out it's mine.

I watch the empty window. Where's Ranger? He's no bigger than I am and has no one to give him a leg up. Can he make it?

The ruckus inside gets louder. Dogs bark, people scream,

then a loud bang. My heart freezes. Was that a door, or did they kill my hero, Ranger? That can't be!

My throat swells, choking me. My heart flips, and I'm beside myself with worry when a shaggy shape fills the window and then lands next to me.

Ranger barks.

"You're still here, baby? I held them back as long as possible to give you time to get away!"

That's the sweetest thing that anyone has ever said to me, other than giving me bacon. I'm so touched that I lick Ranger's nose, and he licks mine back.

That's a severe break in protocol. We're supposed to smell each other's butts first, but extreme situations require extraordinary measures.

The door opens, and a flashlight spears the darkness, looking for us. We take off, running shoulder to shoulder, in the great escape of my life.

"Love you, baby," Ranger pants.

My heart pounds. I'm free and in love. I've never felt so young.

14

THE INDIAN SUMMER

What a life! Ranger and I did everything together: we played in the fresh snow, chased squirrels in the park, and rummaged the trashcans for food. I've never had so many food wrappers, chicken bones, and soggy pizza boxes.

Every morning we woke up together to another beautiful day, and every night we curled around each other to gaze at the stars. One night we sheltered under an old porch from the snow, and I told Ranger everything Jones had taught me about snow.

"You know snow is just like rain, only colder? That's why it always melts into water and ends up as mud."

Ranger cocked his head in amazement.

"Wow! That makes a lot of sense. You know, Maddie, it's got to be wonderful to have someone teach you things. I never did. But for a stint in a hospital and another in a kennel, I've lived in the streets for as long as I can remember. The street is my home. It's not always easy, but you're free. You choose where to sleep and when to get up. You decide where to go and what to do. Sometimes you eat, and some-times you don't, but at least you're free. That's important to me."

I cocked my head.

"But what's your mission? What's your responsibility? How do you make the world a better place?"

Ranger shook. Some of his snow fell on my tongue, and I ate it.

"Sorry, baby, but here in the street, where every day could be your last, it's not about responsibility. It's all about survival. I can see how they both matter. But as for how much, it all depends on where you're coming from."

Enchanted days, those were. But then, my need to find Jones overpowered my desire to be with Ranger. I had to go.

"I'm sorry, Ranger. I really care for you, but Jones is my responsibility. I have to make sure he's all right. He has nobody but me."

"How about his daughter?"

"She's a witch. She wanted nothing to do with him until he got sick. Jones warned me about her long ago. 'Watch out, Maddie,' he said. 'That witch will crawl out of her hole and come to grab everything as soon as I can't defend myself. Don't let her.'

"I promised I'd keep him safe, look after him, and make sure he dies in his own bed, but I didn't. I have to go."

Ranger sighed.

"You're breaking my heart, Maddie. German or not, you're the most beautiful girl I've ever met. I'll always miss you."

My throat tightened.

"Thanks, Ranger."

We licked each other's noses one more time, and I left.

My heart was frozen and my paws heavy like lead as I headed home. I needed to find Gwen and follow her to Jones.

By the time I found the mailbox, my paws were frozen and my heart was heavy. I'll do a quick check, then catch a nap under the maple trees and wait for Gwen, I thought. But then I caught a whiff of Jones.

Really?

I peeked through the dining room window. There he was, lying in his recliner, talking to Gwen. I knew it was him even without sniffing his crotch because he wore his old sweater, the one Red ate a hole in. But he wasn't happy.

"Don't even think about it. I'm not going anywhere. This is my home," he said.

"But Father..."

"Don't even go there. Where's my stuff? Where are my books? And more importantly, where's Maddie?"

Gwen put her hands on her hips.

"You can't take care of a dog. You can't even take care of yourself. You can barely transfer from your chair to your bed."

"That's nonsense. I don't take care of Maddie. She takes care of me. And, unlike you, she makes me happy. Where is she?"

Gwen sighed.

"She's gone."

"What?"

"I tried to find her a home, but nobody wanted an old dog. So I took her to a shelter. But a few days ago, they left me a message to tell me she was gone."

"Gone? My Maddie? You killed my Maddie, you witch?"

"I didn't kill her. And don't talk to me like that. I'm your only daughter. She was nothing but a useless dog."

Jones turned purple. He pushed himself up to his feet and leaned on his walker.

"Get lost, you witch. You killer! I don't want to ever see you again."

"Now, now, Father. You know you need someone to look after you. And you shouldn't be standing. That's not good for your hip."

She pushed him. He fell back into his recliner with a yelp.

That was all I could take. I raced to the dog door, squeezed into the mudroom, dashed into the living room, and barked.

"Get lost, you witch. Go away!"

Gwen stared at me like she'd seen a ghost.

"But they said...."

"Maddie!"

Jones opened his arms. I jumped on him and licked his face, and he hugged me and kissed my muzzle. I licked his tears, and he scratched my ears.

Gwen pursed her lips.

"How you can even imagine that dog can take care of you is beyond me. You can't walk, can't drive, can't shop. All you do is lay in your bed feeling sorry for yourself all day."

Jones shook his head.

"Grab your broom and fly away, Gwen. All these years, I hoped you'd grow up to become a human someday, but I was wrong. Get lost."

Gwen's glare told me she'd happily kill us both. She took a step towards Jones, but I raised my hackles, bared my teeth, and growled like a Porsche with a broken muffler.

"Don't you take another step!"

Gwen stepped back. She grabbed her fur coat and snarled.

"Good luck with your mutt. You don't deserve any better. Don't expect me to even light a candle when you die."

Jones laughed.

"Go away and don't come back."

That night, as I lay in Jones's bed with my head on his chest and listened to him snore, I felt sad but relieved. I missed Ranger, but I'd gotten back home and done my job.

But boy, aren't humans weird? None of my kids would ever treat me like Gwen had treated Jones. But my kids aren't human, of course. They're better than that.

15

HOT DOGS AND SECOND CHANCES

It took a while, but the days got longer, the snow melted, and the trees bloomed. Jones's hip got better, and he started walking again. As he got stronger, we walked a little further every day. I sniffed the breeze, and Jones waved to the neighbors as I barked at their cats. I never forgot to sniff the mailbox and squat to leave Ranger a message in case he stopped by. I hadn't seen him since I returned home, but every now and then, I found a peemail telling me that he missed me. I missed him too.

I had a little trouble with the steps as we walked back. Jones frowned.

"You doing OK, Maddie? You're getting a bit chubby. We need to walk more."

It didn't help. As days went by, I got bigger and bigger. Jones didn't know what to think until he put his hands on my belly and felt the life inside.

His eyes grew wide.

"Really, Maddie? We're gonna have puppies?"

"Really."

"Who...who are they going to look like?"

I didn't quite know how to say it, so my ears flattened a little.

"Their father's a golden retriever named Ranger, who helped me escape from the kennel. He's a hero and a free dog."

Jones nodded.

"Wow. I'd love to meet him someday."

Me too. We, German shepherds, aren't particularly prone to melancholy, but my charmed days with Ranger will be forever in my heart. I'd love to get a chance to tell him about the snow, the stars, and so many things we never got to talk about.

But he has his life, and I have mine.

Then, one day, my belly took on a life of its own, squeezing itself inside out. Jones kneeled by my shoulder and stared at my tail.

"Push, Maddie. Push."

I pushed and pushed.

Blue came out. Then Green, Brown, Black, White, and Yellow.

There was no Red.

I'd just cleaned up the kids and was watching them raid the milk bar when someone barked outside.

"Maddy? May I come?"

I glanced at Jones. "That's Ranger."

Jones opened the door.

"Come in, Ranger."

Ranger stuck his nose in and glanced at Jones. He sniffed high and low, then shuffled in, his tail a little low.

I sniffed him, and my heart melted. He's just as handsome as I remembered, with his shaggy coat and crooked tail. And he smells like he's rolled in dead fish.

"This is for you, Maddie," he says, dropping a hot dog under my nose.

That's the nicest gift I ever got. I know that Ranger stole it just for me, and I'm so touched that I don't know whether to lick his nose or the hot dog. I'm still wondering when he licks my nose and goes to sniff the puppies. He checks them one by one, then wags his tail in approval.

"I'm so proud of you, Baby. They're the most beautiful sight I've ever seen. Other than you, of course."

He's lying, of course. The pups are blind, deaf, and bald. Even worse, they're orange, instead of dark, like all my other litters. But I love them just the same.

"Thank you, Ranger."

He licks my nose again and wags his tail at Jones. He heads to the door as Jones wipes his nose with the sleeve of his half-eaten sweater.

"Ranger, would you like to join us for dinner?" Jones asks.

Ranger stares at him, then at me with wide eyes. I bet it's his first dinner invite, so I wag my tail to encourage him.

"Great idea, Jones. What's for dinner?"

"Meatloaf with mashed potatoes and vanilla ice cream."

I cock my head and look at Ranger over the pups raiding the milk bar.

"Will you stay, please?"

Ranger tucks his tail between his legs. I know he's terrified to be locked in. He'd love to run, but, like the hero he is, he sighs and licks my nose.

"Whatever you say, my dear."

AFTERWORD

Dear reader,

Thank you for reading my book. I hope you enjoyed reading it as much as I loved writing it. If you did, please **take a minute to leave a review** and tell a friend. That would help other readers find it and enjoy it too, and I'd really appreciate it.

If you'd like to read more, go to my website, **RadaJones.com** for a really lovely surprise, and to sign up for my updates and freebies. Drop me a line if you feel like it. I'd love to hear from you.

Rada

ABOUT THIS BOOK

This book is a work of fiction. As you may know, dogs don't write much other than peemail and publish even less. They can read our souls, but their spelling is nothing to write home about.

That's why I wrote Mom's story, a love story to Sake, the short-legged mutt I found in a ditch when I was six.

She was beautiful to me, though Mother said she was ugly. Still, she allowed me to keep her, and Sake was my best friend and only confident through my harsh childhood and teenage years. She shared my food, made me laugh, and licked my tears.

I relished in every one of her puppies, watched them open their eyes and learn the world, and cried with her when they left. Then we started over.

Sake taught me that love never ends.

Rada

BOOKS BY RADA JONES

BECOMING K-9: A Bomb Dog's Memoir

BIONIC BUTTER: A Three-Pawed K-9 Hero

K-9 VIPER: The Veteran's Story

LOVELY K-9: A Prison Puppy

K-9 RAMBO: The Dutch Master

K-9 PROZAK: POW

<u>MOM</u>: A Dog Story Prequel to BECOMING K-9

<u>**K-9 HEROES, Books 1, 2, 3**</u>

OVERDOSE: An ER Phycological Thriller

(ER Crimes: The Steele Files Book 1)

MERCY: An ER Thriller

(ER Crimes: The Steele Files Book 2)

POISON: An ER Thriller

(ER Crimes: The Steele Files Book 3)

STAY AWAY FROM MY ER, and Other Fun Bits of Wisdom

ER CRIMES: The Steele Files

Box Set: Books 1-3

ABOUT THE AUTHOR

Rada Jones was born in Transylvania, near Dracula's Castle. Growing up between communists and vampires taught her that humans are fickle, but one can always depend on dogs and books. That's why she read everything she could find, including the phone book – too many characters, too little action – and took home every stray, from dogs to frogs.

After immigrating to the US, she went to med school and worked in the ER for years, but she still speaks like Dracula's cousin.

When working nights got old, she left the ER to write. Her **ER CRIMES** feature serial killers, some of them really nice people, and Dr. Emma Steele, an ER doc with a deep thirst for red wine. If you're into dark humor, check out her medical essays in **STAY AWAY FROM MY ER.**

But if you're into dogs, the **K-9 HEROES** are right for you.

Check out **RadaJones.com** for updates and freebies.

facebook.com/radajonesmd

twitter.com/JonesRada

instagram.com/RadaJonesMD

bookbub.com/profile/rada-jones

EXCERPT FROM BECOMING K-9
A BOMB DOG'S MEMOIR

Who knew training humans was so hard? You'd wonder why. They aren't that stupid. It takes them a while, but they eventually learn when you want out, you're hungry or you're thirsty. They can even talk to each other by making noise with their tongue. How weird is that? Even my brother Blue, who's the slowest of us all, knows that the tongue is for lapping water and panting to cool down.

Mom cocked her head and licked my nose.

"That's the best they can do, dear. They have no tails, their ears don't move, and most don't even have enough fur to raise their hackles. No wonder they're confused and need us to guide them. And that's what we do; that's our life's work. But we need to choose them carefully."

Mom was on her sixth litter and very wise. Beautiful, too, with her long muzzle, amber eyes, and smooth, shiny fur, all black but for her golden legs and loving pink tongue.

She glanced at Yellow, who chased his tail instead of

paying attention, and growled. He hung his head and sat in line with the rest of us to listen.

It was a lovely summer day as Mom homeschooled us in Jones's front yard. The warm wind tickled my nose. I bit it, but I caught nothing. I tried again, but Mother threw me a side glance, so I closed my mouth and sat still.

"Boys and girls, today's the day. People will come to check you out and choose which one to take home. They don't know it, but it doesn't work that way. You choose your humans, but choose them wisely. Sniff them all, then pick the ones that smell like food if you want a good life. You may sometimes get bacon, maybe even grapes. Humans say dogs don't eat grapes, but that's poppycock. They just want to keep them for themselves. My grandma was a pure-bred Alsatian, and she loved Riesling. I never had Riesling, but Concord isn't bad."

A shiny strip of drool dripped from Mom's mouth. She licked it off and inspected us. We were seven: three boys and four girls. But that doesn't much matter when you're just ten weeks old. The only difference is how you pee. The boys don't know how to squat so they need something to lift their leg to, like a bush or a mailbox. How stupid!

"Why don't you just lift your leg, if that's what you need to do? What does the bush have to do with anything?"

"Leave them alone, Red."

I tried, but it was hard. I was the runt of the litter, so I had to prove myself all the time. Mom said I had a Napoleonic complex.

"What's that?"

"It's when you're the smallest, so you have to be meaner to show them that size doesn't matter."

I told you Mom is brilliant. She came all the way from

Germany when she was just a pup. Our human, Jones, has two passions: German shepherds and history. Mom was his first German shepherd, and he spent lots of time teaching her things most dogs never heard about.

He still does, even now that she's old. He sits in his recliner and reads to her as she lays by the fireplace. Sometimes I listen in. There was a story about a dude named Hitler. Not a nice guy, but for loving German shepherds. Another one about that short guy Napoleon who tried to conquer the world while wearing funny hats. And one about some place called Afghanistan.

"That's a bad war, Maddie," Jones said, scratching the four white hairs in his beard. "Those Taliban, they are not nice people."

He calls her Maddie, but her real name is Madeline Rose Kahn Van Jones. He is Jones. The Van is for Van Gogh, some orange dude who got so mad he bit off his own ear. The rest is just for show, since people pay more for dogs with long names; they call that a pedigree. Mom's pedigree is longer than her tail.

As always, Mom was right. People came to see us, and they brought their spouses, their kids, and even their dogs to check us out and choose which one to get. Like, really? Jones said that only one out of twenty German shepherd owners is smarter than his dog. I don't believe it. I bet he fudged the numbers to feel better. You think you own a dog? Who feeds who? Who cleans after who? Who does the work, everything but making decisions? You, human, in case you didn't know it. You don't buy a dog; you hire supervision. But I digress.

My littermates and I wore colored collars so humans could tell us apart. There was no need, really, since we were all different, but humans couldn't see it. What color did I wear? Red, of course. I was small, but I was the queen of the litter, whether the others liked it or not.

A fat man in a Hawaiian shirt stopped to stare at me. He called his female.

"Look at this red one! Isn't he cute?"

She hobbled closer, leaning on her crooked stick. I love sticks, so I tried to take it. She didn't want to let go, but I insisted. They laughed.

"Let's get him."

Jones cleared his throat.

"Red is lovely, indeed, but she's a very active little person who needs a lot of attention. How much time do you plan to work with her every day?"

"Work with her?"

"Yes. Walk her, train her, and play with her."

They stared at him like he'd lost his marbles. He smiled.

"May I recommend Brown here? He's lovely, easygoing, and eager to please. He'll be happy to lay on the sofa watching TV. Or Miss Green? She's a polite little lady who gets along with everyone and never disappoints."

Brown left. So did Green, Yellow, and even White, while I stayed, waiting for my forever home.

"Take it easy, Red dear," Mother said when there were only two of us left—Black and me. "You need to soften up a bit; otherwise, you'll be left without a family. People look for easygoing dogs to fit into their lives, not for somebody to take charge. Though maybe they should, really, but they aren't smart enough to know that."

Her German accent made her words feel harsh. Have you ever listened to Germans? It's like they're constipated while they also have a cold. They keep clearing their throats, so their words come out like bullets from a machine gun. I don't speak German, but I love watching old war movies with Jones.

"What do you mean, Mom? What should I do?"

"Lick their hands, sweetheart. Wrap yourself around their feet and stare at them like they hung the moon."

"Are you serious?"

"Of course."

"But they're stupid!"

"Come on, Red, don't be so judgmental. You're just a pup, and you have so much to learn. A nice family will give you a good life. They'll love you, play with you, and spoil you. Knowing you have a good, safe home will lift a weight off my soul."

You think I listened? You've got to be kidding.

That's how I ended up in the military.

Read BECOMING K-9

EXCERPT FROM RANGER

THE ESCAPE ARTIST

I think I'm in luck. These two smell like suckers.

I hide behind the bushes, waiting for them to lock their car and head down the path to the camouflaged stand in the forest. I've been here since noon, hoping that someone would show up. Hunters always bring food, and they're too focused on the deer to notice me.

They shuffle down the path, and I follow. The forest around us is alive but quiet. A full moon lights the oaks, throwing twisted shadows over the leaf-covered trail. I step carefully from one shady spot to another, my paws soft as can be. But a whiff of burger hits my nose, and I drool so hard that my tongue hurts and my belly growls. I drop to the ground, scared that the humans will hear it, but they're too busy talking and don't give a hoot about what goes on behind them. They only care about killing tonight, so I'm safe.

The old one coughs a thick cough and spits to the side.

"We'd better be careful. Bill said there's a bear around here. He raided their food when they left the blind to dress the deer. Watch your back, he said. You don't want to meet one of them monsters."

The tall one shrugs.

"That's BS like everything Bill says. There are no bears around here. And if they were, they'd be looking for nuts, roots, and berries. They're not hungry enough to bother people. Not yet. Now, if it was February...."

The old man shrugs and pulls his camo jacket closer. He shines his flashlight to check behind the trees.

"I dunno, John. He'd barely had three beers when he told me. He even showed me the cooler, all trashed. Looked like a bear to me."

I fall behind a little to make sure they won't see me. Truth be told, I don't need to keep that close. I can track them all the way to the blind, but I'm so hungry I'm not thinking straight. Last night I had nothing but a couple chicken bones. And nothing the night before that. But hungry or not, I'd better be careful around these humans and their guns.

The humans put the blind on a platform to give them a better line of sight and covered it with dead branches and leaves. They did a good job. Between that and the darkness, you'd have a hard time finding it if it wasn't for the smell. It smells like stress sweat, and beer. And burgers.

I lick my chops and hide behind a fallen tree, watching the tall skinny man limp up the steps. His pants legs ride up, and his left ankle reflects the moonlight. It smells like metal. The old man follows, wheezing and coughing. They drop their packs in the blind, then walk back out to check the mud for hoof tracks and the trees for scars.

"This here's a good one."

Wheezy shines his flashlight on a slender ash tree leaning

over the crossing of the paths. Skinny sprinkles some fake doe scent over the scarred tree and the bushes around it, and they return to their stand. A gust of wind fills my nose with the stench of doe piss. It's is so strong it chokes me, but they don't seem bothered. They ready their guns and settle to wait.

I squeeze under the dwarf cedar behind the blind. Here, I'm out of the wind and safe. They couldn't see me in bright daylight, let alone a cloudy night.

They chat softly and sip on their beers. I don't know what they're saying, and I don't care. All I care about is the cooler.

I wait and wait until Wheezy comes out to pee, all panting and hacking, and I wonder why he's here, freezing his butt in the woods when he has food to eat and a warm home to sleep in. And how can they think that the deer won't notice them, as stupid as deer are? These humans talk, cough, and fart so much I could hear them from the road. And they stink. The smell of their beer and their piss will carry for miles, even though they sprayed themselves with something that reminds me of cedars after the first snowfall. And that's still far away. The leaves have only started changing here, but they already smell like rotten leaves and snow.

Mom was right. There's no way you can't understand humans. And you shouldn't trust them. Never trust anyone but yourself, she said, which served me right my whole life.

Something darts behind the trees. It's a small doe, and she's fast. The humans go quiet, and the feral scent of their stress sweat fills my nose. I wait for them to shoot, but they don't shoot. I wonder why when I see the buck chasing the doe, and a shot blasts the night.

The buck leaps over a dead tree like a bird. He's about to vanish when a second shot finds him. He crashes to the ground, screaming, and rolls in a cloud of scattered leaves. The coppery smell of his blood fills my nostrils as his life pours out of him, and my stomach flips.

I don't like killing. I may get a rat or a squirrel when I have nothing else, but that gives me no joy. Unlike humans, who grin as they take selfies with their kill. Where is the fun in that?

Oh, well. The buck is dead, and my time has come. I get ready to sneak in and grab the food while the humans fool with the deer.

I wait until they go to check their kill, then squeeze inside the blind to get my food. I can smell it right here in the plastic cooler, but the darn thing is closed, and I can't open it. I try to rip it apart, but it's made of tough stuff, and I'm running out of time. I'll just take it all.

I grab it and run. But it's big and heavy, and it dangles between my legs. I can't run, so I turn sideways and drag it on the ground.

The men hear me and shout. I should drop it and run, but I can't. I'm too hungry. And I may be slow, but they're even slower, between their metal legs and wheezy lungs. So I keep at it. Five more steps and I'll squeeze between the bushes.

A shot rings out. Something cuts my cheek, then stabs me in the chest. I drop the cooler, crash to the ground, and roll in a cloud of leaves like the deer.

They shot me.

My heart pumps like I'm running, but I'm not. I lie on the ground, fighting for my breath. The air whooshes out of me in salty bubbles. I struggle to pant, but I can't get enough air. I try to crawl, but I'm too weak. I drop to the ground.

The humans shuffle closer, their guns ready.

"What the heck is this?" Wheezy asks.

Skinny shines his flashlight in my eyes.

"It's a dog. It's a God damn dog. What on earth is this dog doing here?"

"You're right. It looks like a golden retriever. He's bleeding out."

"Son of a gun. Just what we needed," Skinny says.

Wheezy sighs.

"Let's take him to the vet."

He tries to lift me, but he can't.

"There's no point. It's close to midnight. They're all closed. Plus, we have to deal with the deer. We'll take him in the morning if he makes it."

Wheezy shakes his head.

"I can't. You dress the deer. I'll take him to the emergency vet down the road, then come back to get you. Just help me get him in the car."

They lean over me, and I flash my teeth and growl. I don't want them touching me, and I'm not going anywhere. I'd rather die here, where I lived.

But I'm too weak to breathe, let alone fight. All I can do is gurgle as the humans lay me on a jacket and drag me to their car. I want to run, but I can't even breathe, and I feel my life draining away with my blood.

Sign up at RadaJones.com to get a free copy of RANGER

www.ingramcontent.com/pod-product-compliance
Lightning Source LLC
Chambersburg PA
CBHW030648190726
48286CB00008B/2719